FROG
in the toilet

Matthew Czarnecki

ISBN 978-1-68526-324-9 (Paperback)
ISBN 978-1-68526-327-0 (Digital)

Covenant Books
11661 Hwy 707
Murrells Inlet, SC 29576
www.covenantbooks.com

To my children. God always has a purpose.

Despite the morning showers, the kids were not dismayed. Every Friday, after lunch, they all went out to play.

After recess was finished, the students went back to class. Grant always ran ahead because he was so fast!

He went into the restroom to wash his messy hands.
Suddenly, there was a sound he could not understand.

"Why is there a noisy splash coming from the stall?"
He went to look and could not believe it at all!

4

There's a huge frog in the toilet!" they heard Grant exclaim. Every student started screaming. It was just insane!

Grant sprinted to the classroom to explain what he had found. The kids thought, *Why is a frog in the toilet splashing around?*

Zane shouted, "The frog is an alien!"

"He arrived with a rocket from deep in outer space."
"He flew into the toilet to find a hiding place."
"I bet the enormous frog wanted to find out
what our school was all about."

Kara thought the frog became lost.

"The frog got misplaced while traveling through the sewer."
"I bet he now wished that his maps app was newer."
"He must have overlooked an important update."
"Then the GPS made him turn left when he should have gone straight."

Ellie started to complain.

"Knowing a frog is in the restroom just makes me so mad!"
"It should not be in the toilet. It belongs on a lily pad."
"It does not matter how the frog got in there. I just want it out!"
"You better take care of this now, or I am going to shout!"

William ignored her and made a joke.

"Maybe he is royalty who just needed a break."
"Suddenly, he transformed into a frog from a lake!"
"There would have been a spell, followed by a boom."
"And it happened here when a prince needed to use the restroom."

Sarah imagined a failed science experiment.

"A scientist tried to send that frog to a lily pad."
"But the teleportation testing went horribly bad."
"The instructions did not get written too neat."
"Suddenly, the frog appeared under the seat."

Ava thought it was Dylan.

"What if he was attempting to trick the entire class?"
"Since we were at recess, he would have had to move fast."
"Imagine Dylan taking that frog out of his bag
and dropping it in the toilet with prankster swag!"

Ellie yelled again!

"Who on earth would purposely touch a frog?"
"Especially one as big as my dog?"
"I'm not kidding this time! Get that crazy frog gone!"
"If you do nothing, I'm going to text my mom!"

Arnold remembered a story he heard.

"Maybe frog came to meet toad, a dear friend,
for a vital friendship he wanted to mend."
"Frog fell into the toilet while searching for his buddy,
wanting to say sorry for mistakenly getting him muddy."

Cole sat there snacking at his desk.

"I do not care why the frog is in there."
Cole's only concern was to eat his lunchbox bare.
Every day, when Cole arrived back to class,
his only goal was to finish lunch at last.

Laughing, Faith said the frog thought he was going for a dip in the pool.

"The frog was trying to take a big leap,
but he tripped over his gigantic feet."
"He splashed right down into the disgusting bowl."
"I bet it was awkward when he lost control."

Moe imagined the frog was a superhero.

"He was protecting pond creatures, flying around,
when he became distracted by the school bell sound."
"The frog fell into our restroom and under the seat is where he landed."
"What if his superpowers got damaged, and now he is left here stranded?"

Nick stated that the frog is a wizard.

"He was trying to speak some mysterious frog magic
when the situation turned terribly tragic."
"As he was attempting to cast his spell,
he slipped, and right into the toilet bowl he fell."

Soon, the students ran out of explanations.

Rejected, Isabelle sighed. "We cannot figure this out."
The children became distraught.
Some began to grumble and pout.
(Except for Ellie, she continued to yell and shout!)
"We just have to know how a huge frog could get in there!"
The teacher reminded them, "Life is not always fair."

He continued.

"You will often face situations you cannot explain."
"Despite this truth, you should never complain."
"Even when life makes us anxious or nervous,
we must believe all things work together on purpose."

Ellie (quite loudly) voiced her opinion again.

"My only request is to move this massive frog away."
"It matters not why the frog is in there today!"
"Someone must remove this vile creature before it's too late."
"What if that frog gets out and makes a daring escape?"

Frogs scare Ellie!

"The frog could jump all around and cause terrifying fright."
"The principal would have to cancel school due to the sight."
"Make a good decision and retrieve that huge frog."
"Release it to the pond and put it on a log."

The teacher asked Grant to check on the frog.

As he went into the stall, Grant surprisingly found an empty toilet!
Dylan spoke. "The frog is now my pet, and I am going to enjoy it!"
"We do not know where he came from, but I will give him my affection."
"This frog will make a splendid addition to my creature collection."

40

Dylan decided to take the frog home!

"After school, I will take this frog. He will ride to my house."
"He can live in an aquarium, next to Cheese, my pet mouse."
"I will name the frog Tad. He is going to be my best friend."
"Now the story of the frog in the toilet will have a peaceful end."

ABOUT THE AUTHOR

Through the years, Matthew Czarnecki has read countless children's stories to his kids before bed and thought, *I could do that!* After a midnight scare of finding an actual frog in his toilet, he often wondered how elementary students might react to such a discovery. Matthew considers the best children's story is one that teaches a valuable life lesson. As the author of *Frog in the Toilet*, Matthew hopes his audience will learn that even though some life situations cannot be explained, everything has a purpose. Matthew is also the husband to an exceptionally captivating woman, a teacher, and a pastor.

CPSIA information can be obtained
at www.ICGtesting.com
Printed in the USA
LVHW051627130622
721139LV00024B/203

9 781685 263249